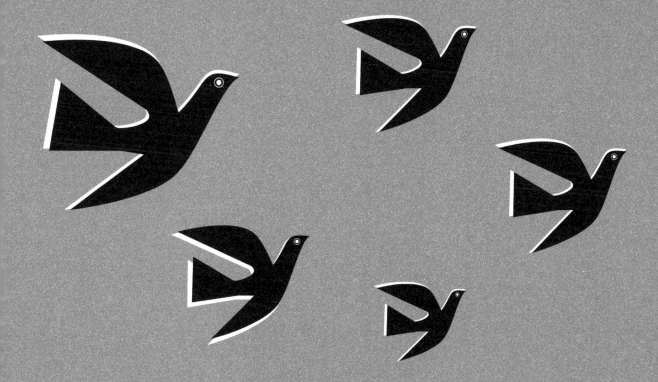

STAY, BENSON!

Thereza Rowe

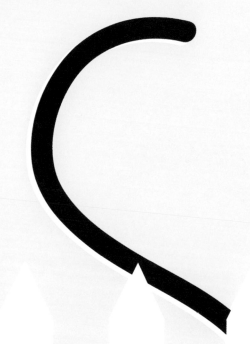

 Thames & Hudson

Every morning before
school, Flick says,

"Be good, Benson.
You **stay** and
watch the house.
No chasing!"

But...

As soon as Flick
waves
goodbye...

...Benson sneaks
out of the
back door...

...and into the garden.

WOOF

WOOF WOOF

WOOF

What did Flick tell you, Benson?

Flick told me,

"Play, Benson!"

MEOW

No, she told you to **stay**, Benson!

But
Benson
digs
under
the
fence...

and the chase begins.

What did Flick tell you?
She told me,

"Play, Benson!"

No, she told you,

"NO
CHASING,
BENSON!"

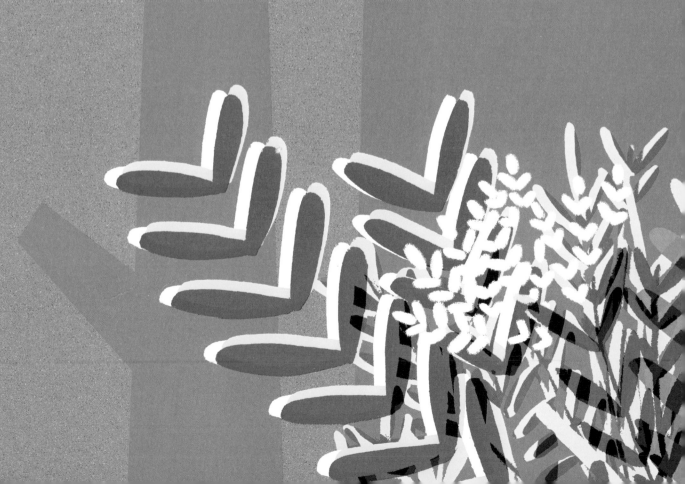

Benson chases the squirrel around the tree

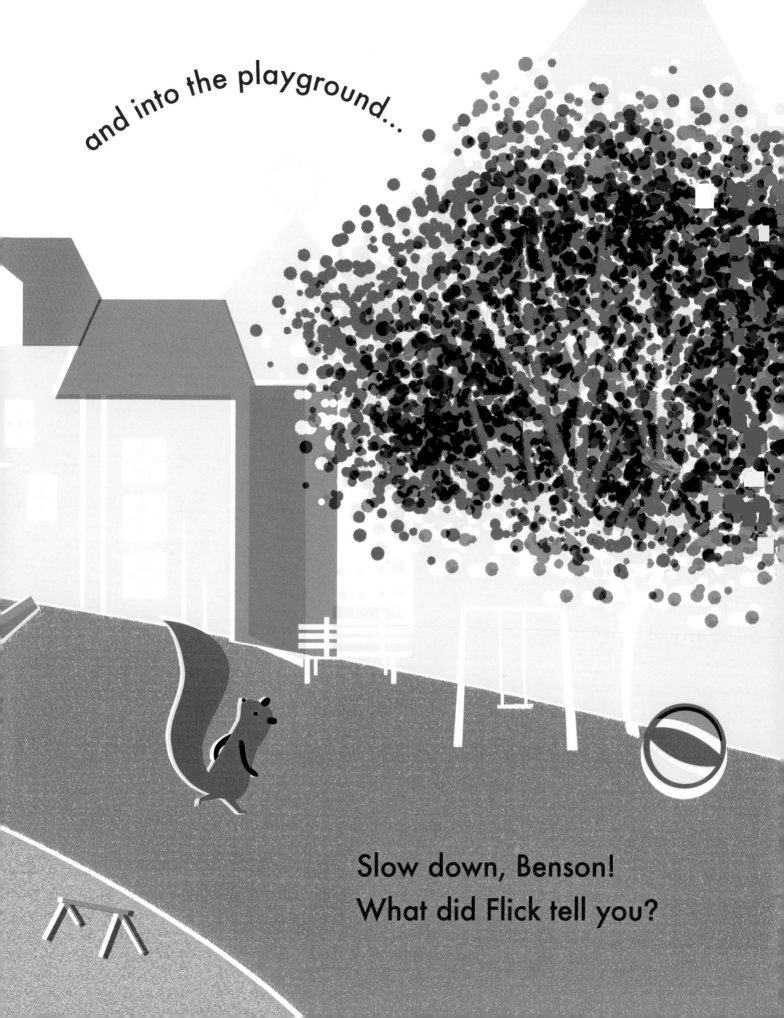

and into the playground...

Slow down, Benson!
What did Flick tell you?

Flick told me, **"Play, Benson!"**

No, she told you to **stay**

and watch the house!

Get out of there, Benson!
Remember Flick told you to be good!

She told me, "Play, Benson!"

That's
enough
Benson!

And watch out for that picnic!

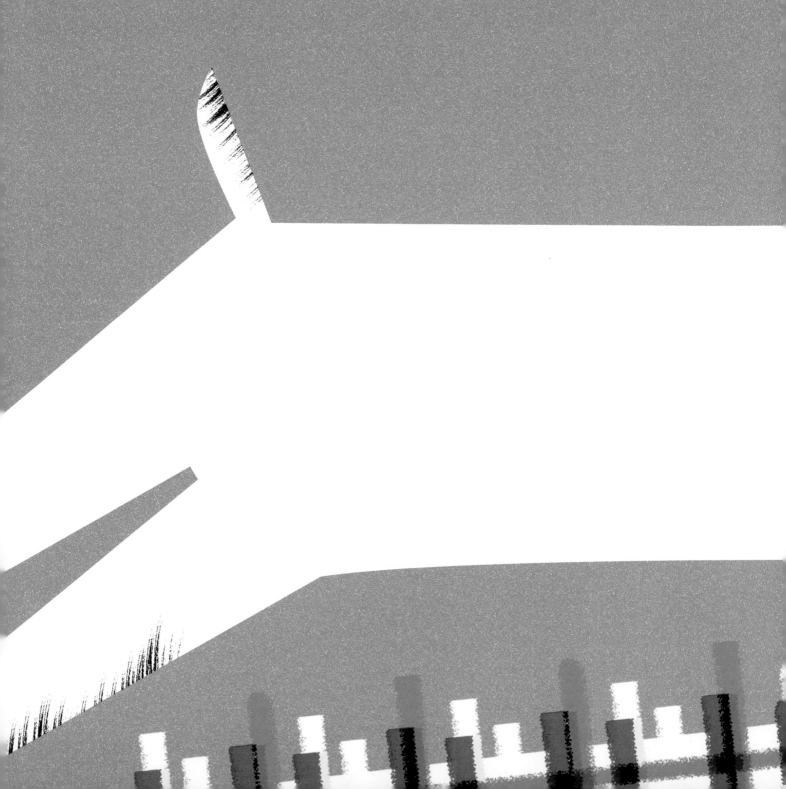

Quick, Quick!

Benson races all the way home
and arrives just in time...

"Have you been a good dog?
Did you **stay**, Benson?"

For Benson, the best dog ever.

First published in the United States of America in 2019 by
Thames & Hudson Inc., 500 Fifth Avenue, New York, New York 10110

www.thamesandhudsonusa.com

Library of Congress Control Number 2018945321

ISBN 978-0-500-65153-7

Printed and bound in China by RR Donnelley